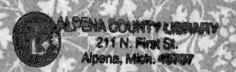

It's snowing outside my window now. Suzanne
is resting on the couch, tender and safe, my affection.
R.S.

Recommended Dewey Decimal Classification: 813
Suggested Subject Heading: AMERICAN FICTION; SHORT STORY
ISBN 1-56476-543-1

Text ©1996 by Penelope J. Stokes
Illustrations ©1996 by Robert Sauber

1 2 3 4 5 6 7 8 9 10 Printing/Year 00 99 98 97 96

Printed in Mexico.

O. HENRY

The GIFT of the MAGI

Adapted by **Penelope J. Stokes**
Illustrated by **Robert Sauber**

**VICTOR BOOKS**

A DIVISION OF SCRIPTURE PRESS PUBLICATIONS INC.
USA CANADA ENGLAND

One dollar and eighty-seven cents. That was all she had. And sixty-two cents of it was in pennies, pennies saved one or two at a time by scrimping and saving and talking the grocer and the butcher and the vegetable man into reducing their prices. Della's cheeks burned at the memory. She hated living this way, trying to stretch every penny until it squealed, and having people around her narrow their eyes and shake their heads with pity, as if they understood the pain her poverty caused.

The truth was, they didn't understand. No one could understand who hadn't lived as Della had lived—saving every possible cent for the past three months, only to come up with one dollar and eighty-seven cents. And tomorrow was Christmas Day. Christmas Day, and she had no money to buy a gift for Jim.

Clutching her dollar and eighty-seven cents in one hand, Della did the only logical thing one could do in such a situation. She flopped down onto the shabby little couch and began to cry—great, wracking howls of anger and frustration and self-pity that, if they couldn't change her situation, at least might make her feel a bit better.

After a while Della's howling subsided into sobs, and the sobs ultimately gave way to sniffles. Even in the midst of her misery, she remembered how her father used to say that life was made up of sobs, sniffles, and smiles—with sniffles predominating. The memory cheered her a little. She sat up, looked around the tiny little apartment, and then went to gaze out the window. She hated being treated as if she were poor, but, in truth, that was exactly what she was. She and her husband, Jim, had little to show for all their hard work—only a small furnished flat at eight dollars a week.

On their mailbox in the hallway downstairs, the name read "Mr. and Mrs. James Dillingham Young"—a rather audacious-sounding title, Della thought, for a couple who subsisted on twenty dollars a

week. The "Dillingham" had been added during a period of prosperity, when Jim was bringing in thirty dollars a week. Now that their income had shrunk to twenty, even the letters on the mailbox had begun to look blurred, as if they were trying to be less conspicuous—perhaps to contract into a modest and unassuming middle initial.

They were poor, all right. But they had happiness. They had love. And they had two possessions which made them feel wealthy, despite their present state of affairs.

The first was Jim's pocket watch. The watch, a legacy from Jim's father and his grandfather before him, was a treasured heirloom. Crafted in gold, with a scripted "Y" engraved on the filigreed cover, it was Jim's pride and joy. If a stranger stopped him on the street to ask the time, Jim would draw it out and open it with a flourish. If it was in his pocket he would finger it lovingly, stroking the fine softness of the gold. He was never without it.

Jim's watch was a masterpiece of craftsmanship. Their other treasure, Della's hair, was a masterpiece of nature. Soft and luxuriant, it fell in shining waves well below her waist. It was her glory and pride—and the envy of every woman who knew her.

If the Queen of Sheba had lived in the flat across the air shaft, Della would have let her hair hang out the window to dry, just to depreciate Her Majesty's jewels and gifts. Had King Solomon been the janitor, with all his treasures piled up in the basement, Jim would have pulled out his watch every time he passed, just to see the old man pluck at his beard with envy. Indeed, they had little in the way of material wealth. One dollar and eighty-seven cents to be exact. But Jim had his watch, and Della had her—

Suddenly Della whirled from the window and went to stand in front of the mirror. Her eyes were shining brilliantly, but her face had gone stark white. Rapidly she pulled down her hair and let it fall to its full length.

Della's hair rippled and shone like a cascade of auburn waters around her. It reached to her knees and wrapped itself about her like a garment. With trembling hands she did it up again, then stood looking into the mirror while a tear slid down her cheek and dropped silently onto the worn carpet.

There was not a moment to lose. Grabbing her old brown hat and her threadbare coat, she headed toward the door.

wisting the buttons on the front of her coat, Della stood in the street and stared up at the sign. *Madame Sofronie*, it read. *Hair Goods of All Kinds. One Flight Up.* Della took the stairs two at a time and flung herself, panting from exertion and fear, in front of the door. She knocked.

No answer.

She knocked again. It was Christmas Eve, after all; perhaps Madame Sofronie was not in. But she had to be in—she just had to be!

At last the door opened, and a well-padded, pasty-faced woman stared down at her. "Well?"

"Will you buy my hair?" Della blurted out breathlessly.

The woman squinted and surveyed her from top to bottom. "I buy hair," she said curtly. "Take off your hat and let's have a sight at the looks of it."

Della stepped into the parlor, whipping off her hat, and deftly removed the pins. The cascade of auburn rippled down, catching the light and shining as if it were alive.

Madame Sofronie lifted the mass of hair with a practiced hand. "Twenty dollars."

Della closed her eyes and took a deep breath. "Give it to me quick," she whispered.

The next two hours were a blur to Della as she ransacked the stores looking for Jim's present. Then, just as she was about to give up in despair, she found it, in a small shop off a dingy back alley.

Surely it had been made for Jim and no one else. There was no other like it in any of the stores she had searched, and she had turned all of them inside out. It was a gold and platinum fob chain—simple in design, proclaiming its value by substance and simplicity alone, not by ornamentation. It was even worthy of The Watch.

As soon as she held its weight in her hands, she knew that it must have been created just for Jim. It was like him, marked by quietness and value—a simple, rich, understated elegance. Now he could display his watch proudly in any company; he no longer had to be shamed by the worn leather strap that he had always used in place of a chain.

Twenty-one dollars they took from her, and, with eighty-seven cents in her pocket, she hurried through the streets toward their flat.

When Della reached home, excitement gave way to reason—and a bit of fear. She took one look at herself in the mirror, and then got out her curling irons and went to work repairing the damage.

Within forty minutes, her head was covered with tiny close curls that made her look a bit like a short-cropped show girl. She set aside the curling irons and looked at her reflection with a critical eye.

"If Jim doesn't kill me before he takes a second look at me," she murmured to herself, "he'll say I look like a Coney Island chorus girl. But what could I do—oh, what could I do with a dollar and eighty-seven cents?"

By seven o'clock, the coffee was made and the chops were frying in the big skillet on the back of the stove. Della doubled the fob chain into her hand and took up a position on the corner of the table near the door.

Jim was never late, and tonight was no exception. When she heard his footsteps on the stairway, her heart began to pound. Della had a habit of saying little silent prayers about the simplest everyday things, and now she whispered, "Please, God, make him think I am still pretty."

The door opened, and Jim stepped in and closed it behind him. He looked thin and very serious, and Della noticed that his overcoat was sadly frayed and he wore no gloves. For the first time she realized what a burden it must be for him—only twenty-two—and bearing the responsibility of caring for a wife.

As soon as Jim stopped inside the door, he froze. His eyes were fixed upon Della, and there was an expression in them that she could not read. It was not anger, or surprise, or disapproval, or horror, or any of the emotions she had been prepared for. He simply stared at her.

"Jim, darling," she cried, jumping off the table and running toward him. "Don't look at me that way. I had my hair cut off and sold it because I couldn't bear to face Christmas without being able to give you a present. It will grow out again—it grows awfully fast. You don't really mind, do you? I had to do it—I just had to. You can't imagine what a beautiful gift I've gotten for you—"

"You've cut off your hair?" Jim asked, the words coming out laboriously, as if he had still not comprehended the fact that Della's beautiful hair was gone.

"Cut it off and sold it," she said. "Don't you love me just as much without it? I'm still me without my hair, just as much as with it."

Jim looked around the room curiously. "You say your hair is gone!" he repeated, with an air almost of idiocy.

"You don't need to look for it," Della said. "It's sold, I tell you—sold and gone—and it went for you." She searched his face anxiously. Somehow, she had to find a way to assure him that she was still his Della, with the hair or without. "It's Christmas Eve, Jim," she went on in a rush, feigning a light laugh. "Maybe the hairs of my head were numbered, but nobody could count my love for you." She took a deep breath. "Now, shall I finish making dinner? The chops are nearly done—"

Jim shook his head as if coming out of a deep sleep. His arms went around Della, and he held her close, stroking her close-cropped hair. "The Magi brought gifts to the Christ Child," he murmured, "valuable gifts. But none of them could compare with ours."

Della leaned back and looked up at him. "What do you mean?"

He released her and reached into his pocket. "Dell," he said softly, "make no mistake about me. Nothing could make me love you any less, not even if you were completely bald. But—" He drew his hand from his pocket and laid a small package on the table. "If you'll unwrap that, you'll understand my reaction."

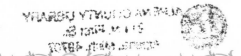

With a squeal of delight, Della fumbled at the paper and unwrapped the gift. When she saw the contents, she let out a joyful cry which quickly turned to tears. For there, inside the clumsily-wrapped parcel, lay The Combs— the set of hair combs she had gazed at in a shop window on Broadway, the combs she had wished for. They were pure tortoise shell with jeweled rims, just the right shade to wear in her beautiful hair. They were expensive, she knew, and her heart had simply longed for them without any hope of possession. Now they were hers, but the tresses they should have adorned were gone.

Still, she hugged them to her, and when she finally had her tears under control, she looked up at him with a smile. "My hair grows so fast, Jim!"

Then, remembering, she leaped up like a singed cat. Jim had not yet seen his beautiful present. She held it out to him eagerly upon her open palm, and the gold and platinum seemed to flash with a reflection of her own bright spirit.

"Isn't it a dandy, Jim? I hunted all over town to find it. You'll have to look at the time a hundred times a day now. Give me your watch, I want to see how it looks—"

She looked up to find him smiling down upon her—a curious smile, as if he possessed a wonderful secret. "Dell," he said, "let's put our Christmas presents away and keep them awhile. They're too nice to use just now."

Suddenly she understood, and tears welled up in her eyes again. "You sold it," she said quietly. "You sold your watch to buy the combs for me."

Still smiling, he tumbled down on the couch and put his hands behind his head. "And you sold your hair to buy the fob chain for me." He reached out, pulled her to himself, and embraced her tenderly. "It's the finest gift I could ever imagine," he said. "Except for you, my dearest Dell. You are my most precious treasure, you know."

Della looked deep into his eyes and kissed him. "I know," she whispered. "And you are my gift." She drew closer to him and laid her head on his chest. "Merry Christmas, Jim," she sighed. "I've never felt so wealthy in all my life."

The Magi, as everyone knows, were wise men—wonderfully wise men—who brought gifts to the Christ Child in the manger. They invented the art of giving Christmas presents. Being wise, their gifts were no doubt wise as well—carefully selected, and of great value.

Maybe the gifts that Della and Jim chose were not so wise. Perhaps they were only poor, foolish children who unwisely sacrificed for each other the greatest treasures of their house. But let it be known that of all who give and receive gifts, these two were the wisest. They understood Christmas as people rarely understand it. They are the wise ones. They are the Magi.

AFTERWORD

The Gift of the Magi is a story which reflects O. Henry's own struggles with poverty and injustice—and, perhaps, his own experience of the power of love. Jim and Della have little to show for all their hard work, and yet they possess a treasure more priceless than Jim's gold watch or Della's beautiful hair—their love for one another. That love leads them to a kind of self-sacrifice that is rarely seen in this world. They give up their most valued possessions for the good of the other, and they do it willingly and joyfully, without remorse or resentment. In the world's eyes, such sacrifice might be viewed as sheer foolishness, but to them it is the only reasonable response to their commitment to one another. This kind of loving sacrifice, O. Henry says without apology or explanation, is true wisdom—the gift of the Magi, who worshiped the newborn Christ with the best they had to offer.

O. HENRY
[William Sydney Porter]

O. Henry was born William Sydney Porter on September 11, 1862, at Polecat Creek, near Greensboro, North Carolina. Like many of the characters he created in his stories, his life was marked both by sadness and promise. At the age of three he lost his mother to tuberculosis; in his twenties he endured the deaths of both his newborn son and namesake, and the grandmother who had raised him.

In his thirties, just as he had begun to break into publishing, using the name O. Henry and other pseudonyms, he suffered additional setbacks, including the loss of his wife to tuberculosis. Eventually he moved to New York City, remarried, and published more then ten collections and hundreds of individual short stories. O. Henry returned to his mountain roots only after his death in 1910; he is buried in Asheville, North Carolina, at the Riverside Cemetery overlooking the French Broad River.